CW00420217

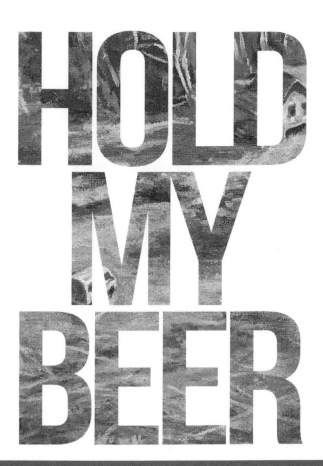

HOLD MY BEER

AN APOCALYPSE

Fr. Mark Goring, CC

ISBN: 9798520657439

Edited by Dawn Slawecki

Interior layout: Sr. Michael Penelope Nguyen, SC
            servantsofthecross.ca

Cover painting: Isaac MacDonald
            isaacmacdonaldart.com

Cover design: Oswaldo Perez
            jaroz.com

This book is dedicated to
all those who hope
to enjoy a drink
with me in
Heaven.

Contents

Chapter 1

A Place to Hide

"The internet is down and cell phones aren't working. The conference speakers who flew out last night never made it home. The only channel available is state run news," Ralph summarizes the situation for us as we near the airport.

"Government media is reporting a coordinated terrorist attack on major communications facilities around the world," Christie adds.

"I'm not sure I want to get dropped off," Texas says. "We might need to find a place to hide."

I grip the steering wheel of my old grey church van.

"How about I loop around once? If something seems amiss, we can go into town and try to sort things out." I look into the rear-view mirror and can see that my five American passengers are agreeable to my proposal.

"My church is not far from here. We can go there. Maybe our phones will start working again," I say, trying to sound optimistic.

"Okay," Ralph responds.

Ralph is sitting next to me in the passenger seat. He has a coffee in one hand and a donut in the other. He is a New Yorker. Ralph produces a weekly podcast called *The Ralph Report*, which offers conservative commentary. He is what some Catholics would call a Traditionalist, who attends the Latin Mass. Ralph is in his late fifties, somewhat overweight, with unkempt grey hair.

"Father Pedro, do you think they are arresting people?" Christie asks me.

"I hope not," I reply. "But no one who flew out last night seems to have made it home," I remind her.

"How far are we from the US border?" Christie asks me.

"About an hour," I answer.

Christie is a beautiful African American woman from Detroit. She is in her mid-twenties and is a journalist for the *Pro-Life News Service*. She has shoulder-length, curly hair and is of average height. She is a convert to Catholicism from Pentecostalism.

I drive slowly through the passenger drop-off area. We all look into the airport terminal through the large, sliding glass doors. Everything seems normal. In the drop-off lanes, people are pulling suitcases out of trunks, hugging loved ones goodbye, and tugging roller bags into the terminal. I move on without stopping. As we drive away from the terminal, we see a line of five military trucks behind a fence, close to the runway. Uniformed men are standing next to a terminal door. Some of them are holding machine guns. Two men in brown robes are being led into one of the trucks. They appear to be in handcuffs.

"The Franciscan Friars!" Texas exclaims.

Texas is, oddly enough, from Arizona. He is tall, has sandy blond hair and is in his early twenties. His YouTube channel, Extremely Catholic, is popular among young people. Texas produces adventure videos with his wild and crazy Catholic friends.

"I had beer and pizza with those two guys two nights ago," Texas says.

"Oh! What's going on? What's going on?" Christie asks. She strains her neck to take in the disturbing scene.

"Perhaps we should go to your church," Mother Elijah calmly suggests.

Mother Elijah is a nun from Louisiana. She is a well-known sister who has authored a number of books on Christian spirituality. Mother Elijah is tall and slender and in her sixties. She wears a white and blue religious habit. She has beautiful blue eyes and radiates a wonderful peace.

"Does anyone want to be dropped off?" I ask, looking into my rear-view mirror.

All five of my passengers decline, and so we drive away from the airport.

***

The Kingdom Media Conference happens every October in Ottawa, Canada. The event is live-streamed all over the world, and features some of the most influential Catholics working in media. The conference ended with a large banquet last night that was open to the public. The organizers asked me to celebrate the closing Mass for the event. They thought it would be nice if a newly ordained local priest was part of the conference. I also helped with some of the practical details of the conference. My last two tasks are to shuttle these five VIP guests to the airport and then deposit the cash from the conference registrations at the bank.

***

As we make our way down the parkway, into the city, a slight drizzle begins. I turn on the windshield wipers. I look into the rear-view mirror to check on my passengers.

"What time did cell phones stop working?" Brother Dominic asks.

Dominic, originally from Vermont, is a religious friar with the Order of Preachers, more commonly known as the Dominicans. He is in his late thirties and is probably the most highly respected Catholic on social media. His knowledge of scripture, the Church Fathers,

St. Thomas Aquinas, theology, philosophy, history, literature and just about every other area of knowledge is staggering. For years he has been posting videos on a wide range of topics that are always clear, concise, and excellently produced. Dominic wears the white Dominican medieval habit. He is of average height and thin, with deep set brown eyes and carefully combed black hair.

"They are saying it was at 2 AM," Texas answers.

"And we lost television and the internet at the same time?" Dominic inquires.

"Yes," Christie answers. "The hotel receptionist told me that the TV started broadcasting again at 4 AM. Only one channel, though — *News Nation*."

"And they're calling it an orchestrated terrorist attack," Ralph says, shaking his head.

"*News Nation* is run by the Canadian government?" Dominic asks me.

"Pretty much," I answer.

"Communications systems are down but flights aren't being cancelled and Franciscans are being arrested. It's pretty obvious what this is," Ralph tells us and takes a swig of coffee.

Chapter 2

Conspiracy Reality

We drive down a quiet street towards my church. The rain has stopped and the sun is shining brightly. Ottawa, Canada's capital city, is beautiful this time of year. The trees are bursting with color. In the rectory, I make tea for my five guests as we try to sort out our situation.

Dominic and Mother Elijah are sitting together on one couch, both sipping tea in the most proper manner. Dominic in his white Dominican robes sitting next to Mother Elijah in her white and blue religious habit is a beautiful sight. Christie and Ralph are sharing another couch. Seeing these two next to each other is more of an amusing sight. Both are slouching and not drinking their tea. Texas walks around examining the pictures and knickknacks in the room.

"You play soccer?" Texas asks as he looks at a team picture on the wall.

"Yes. That was our team in the seminary," I say.

"When I saw you the other day, my first thought was 'This young priest sure looks like a soccer player.'" Texas tells me. "You've got that short stocky build that so many soccer players have. As a matter of fact, you kind of look like Oswaldo—you know, from Mexico?"

I chuckle. "My mom is from Mexico," I tell him.

Mother Elijah, Christie, Dominic, and Ralph are quiet. They don't seem interested in soccer at the moment.

***

"This is definitely the Media Reset," Ralph tells us.

"I'm surprised it's taken this long," Dominic says.

"God is still in charge," Mother Elijah comments.

"So does that mean we're supposed to destroy our phones and anything else the Globies can use to track us?" Christie asks.

"Yup," Texas answers. "And we're going to have to go into hiding," he adds.

"Father Pedro, have you given any thought to a good hideout for us?" Ralph asks me.

My five guests seem to know exactly what is going on. I am shocked at how nonchalantly they speak about it.

"I thought that was just a conspiracy theory," I say.

Ralph scoffs. Christie rolls her eyes. Texas laughs. Dominic and Mother Elijah look at me with pity.

***

The Media Reset is a so-called conspiracy theory that many have been warning about for the last couple of years. The theory claims that there are global powers who want to reorganize the world's economic structures so that a small number of people control all the world's wealth. They call this the New World Order. Conspiracy theorists believe that most of the mainstream media is controlled by the world's elite, who are using the media to advance their agenda. A day will come, many have warned, when the global communications infrastructure will go down due to a supposed terrorist attack. When the communications systems are restored, only media sources supportive of the New World Order will be able to operate. This is what conspiracy theorists call the Media Reset.

Some have been making efforts to warn people about this alleged global takeover. Many have taken to social media to speak out against this attempt to take away free speech and silence dissenting voices. Conspiracy theorists call the global elite "Globies." The term has become popular even among the general population.

Conspiracy theorists also claim that concentration camps have been built all over the world to detain people who resist the Globies. Governments typically call these facilities "health centers" or "job training centers." People are placed in these facilities, against their will, if the government decides a person is "sick" or needs "job training."

Most of the population does not resist this New World Order, according to conspiracy theorists, because the Globies promise financial security. All will be provided for by the government and working will become optional.

"I've had my doubts about this whole Media Reset thing," I tell my guests, "but I can't deny that something really weird is going on."

"The Globies aren't going to be waiting for us to figure this out," Ralph warns. "We need to disappear and we need to disappear fast," he says.

The rest of my guests nod in agreement.

***

I begin to think of different possibilities for hiding out. "All of our religious houses are out of the question. The Globies will look for us there," I say. "My brother has a camper on a lake, but it's small and there are too many people close by."

"Oh, this is crazy!" Christie exclaims.

"I think I know someone who can help us," I say.

KNOCK, KNOCK.

We are all startled and look towards the hallway. I get up and make my way to the front door.

"Helen, is everything all right?" I ask.

Helen is an older parishioner who lives across the street from the church. She seems a little distressed.

"Father Pedro," Helen says to me in a loud whisper, "Nick sent me. The police are looking for you and your friends. An announcement was sent out on the police radio. He said your name is on the list. You need to hide!" she warns me.

I walk back into the front room and can see that my guests have heard everything.

"Her husband is a police officer. They're looking for us," I tell them. "I have a friend who lives alone on a farm three hours north of here. I trust him and he is not someone who anyone would suspect of helping me," I say.

"What's your friend's name?" Mother Elijah asks.

"Mr. Mister," I answer.

Christie holds back a laugh. "Mr. Mister?" she asks.

"That's what everyone calls him," I reply.

"Does Mr. Mister own guns?" Texas asks.

I look Texas in the eyes and in a lowered voice respond, "He owns guns."

Texas nods.

***

I am wearing my formal priestly attire with my Roman collar and so I change into civilian clothing. Dominic and Mother Elijah do the same. We destroy our phones, withdraw as much cash as possible from a bank machine and then destroy our credit cards and anything else the Globies might be able to use to track us.

We start our journey driving south for a while so that traffic surveillance cameras will give the impression our old grey van is headed towards the southern border. Once south of the city and in the country, we turn off the main road and take rural roads that lead us north towards Mr. Mister's farm. Two hours later, we are a good piece north of the city in the beautiful remote countryside of Quebec. There is a sense of relief that we have escaped the city and have not been caught by the Globies. None of us, however, has any idea what the future holds for us, or for the world.

***

It's late afternoon and we've been driving for over three hours. I can't remember exactly which driveway leads to Mr. Mister's farm. The road has many little turnoffs. Some are logging roads, others lead to cottages or hunt camps, others seem to lead nowhere. There are hardly any road signs in this area. I make a third stop, checking to see if this might be the right driveway. My passengers aren't complaining but must be getting impatient with my inability to remember exactly where Mr. Mister lives.

"I think this is it," I say, as I turn into the driveway.

"That's what you said the last two times," Christie responds.

I drive cautiously down the winding gravel path and try to remember some distinctive features of Mr. Mister's homestead.

"They're all the same," I say in frustration.

I bring the van to a stop, ready to turn around.

Mother Elijah, who has been silent for a long while, says in a low voice, "Why is that man pointing a gun at us?"

Chapter 3

Shotgun Visit

We all look to the passenger side of the van, the side on which Mother Elijah is sitting. An older man wearing a ball cap stands ten feet away, pointing his shotgun towards us. I press the power window button to lower the passenger window where Ralph is sitting.

"Get the hell off of my land," the man says firmly.

"You couldn't hit the broad side of a barn with that rusty old pipe," I respond.

The man lowers his gun and looks at me.

"Father Pedro! Good to see you," he says with a smile.

***

Mr. Mister lets me park the van in his old barn, about a hundred yards from his house.

The walk to the farmhouse is quite pleasant after sitting for hours in the van. Our vehicle is parked out of sight and for the first time I feel somewhat safe. Mr.

Mister is carrying his shotgun over his shoulder with one hand and has a beer in the other.

"You guys out on some kind of a road trip?" he asks.

"Not exactly," I respond. I begin to tell him about the Kingdom Media Conference, and introduce him to my five guests.

"This is Mother Elijah from Louisiana," I start.

"Just call me Sister," Mother Elijah says.

"Nice to meet you, Sister," Mr. Mister says.

"This is Texas. He's from Arizona."

Mr. Mister gives Texas a puzzled look.

"Ralph here is from New York and Dominic is from Vermont," I say.

Mr. Mister gives them both a nod.

"And this is Christie from Detroit," I continue.

Mr. Mister holds out his beer to Christie. "Hold my beer," he tells her.

Christie hesitantly takes his beer as he raises his gun and fires a shot. Everyone jumps except Texas.

"Nice shot!" Texas says, and begins to walk into the woods in the direction of Mr. Mister's shot. A moment later Texas comes back carrying a massive bird with one wing still flapping.

"Hope you guys can stay for dinner," Mr. Mister says. "We're having wild turkey tonight."

***

Mr. Mister's farmhouse is old. The home has the smell of wood fire and country cooking. The cookstove and timber walls make it feel like we've just stepped back a hundred years.

"Can I offer you ladies a glass of wine?" Mr. Mister asks Mother Elijah and Christie.

"Oh, yes!" Christie answers.

After pouring each of the ladies a glass of white wine, Mr. Mister grabs four bottles of beer out of the fridge. He twists the top off of the first beer and places it in Ralph's hand, then proceeds to do the same for Dominic and Texas, and finally hands one to me.

"You guys make yourselves at home. I'm going to clean our turkey and get us some supper going," says our gracious host.

Texas follows Mister out the door, presumably wanting to be part of the experience of cleaning the freshly killed game.

***

Over dinner, I explain to Mr. Mister the full story of the internet and phone reception dropping, evidence of people being arrested at the airport, the police announcement on the radio, and how we destroyed our phones and disposed of anything that could be used to track us.

"One of my daughters has been talking about all of this," Mr. Mister responds.

We are all enjoying the thin strips of wild turkey Mr. Mister fried in butter and spiced with a Montreal chicken spice. We have all been eating beans from the big pot simmering on the stove, and Ralph, Texas, and Dominic have been helping themselves to second and third servings.

"This is delicious," Christie comments. "What kind of meat is in the beans?"

"Save some room for dessert," Mr. Mister announces. "I've got some fresh apple pie. Apples are from the trees out back," he proudly states. "I had a big black bear going after my apples this year," Mr. Mister adds. "That's where she is now," nodding at the pot of beans.

***

After dinner, we continue to ponder the gravity of the situation and consider our options. Mr. Mister explains to us that his daughter plans to visit him with her family in a few days and that our best option would be to find a cottage or a hunting camp in which to hide out for a while. He begins to consider different camps as possible hideouts.

"The Ryersons have a camp on Papineau creek. They got three moose out of there this year. Hendrix has a camper on the north end of The Lane but it's not insulated. Too small for your crew. Ricky's gang has a nice place on Osborn but they got into some drinking and the place caught fire. The whole east wall got charred and still hasn't been fixed. The lads from Five Cent Club have their camp by Blake Falls but they're up there with the sleds all winter fishing walleye. Ernie got a nice eight pounder by the big rock last winter. Keith and his boys were using the old lodge by Trevor Lake. He cut off his leg sawing spruce up there last year. His boys will be going for partridge till the snow is deep."

Texas and Ralph are in awe of how Mr. Mister can rhyme off specific details of the region's various hunt camps. Christie and Mother Elijah both seem disturbed by some of the details Mr. Mister finds it necessary to include.

"You could stay at Monsignor Pat's camp up by Gene," Mr. Mister finally states. "Trevor and five other guys just closed the place after the hunt, and not too many people go up that way," he adds.

Mr. Mister looks at me as though he's waiting for my opinion. I don't know how to respond.

"Is there good hunting up there?" Texas asks.

"They got one moose this year. A cow moose. Jay-Jay took the shot from 130 yards with his new 306. Remington bolt. She was in the far bay. Hit her just above the shoulder. The lads had to track her for nearly two hours. They followed the trail of blood and when they finally found her..."

"Would we be able to stay in this camp for a little while?" Mother Elijah interrupts with a slightly raised voice.

19

"Yes, I think that's your best bet. I can talk to the Monsignor and let him know you're up there. I'm sure he'll be okay with it, and he'll keep things quiet," Mr. Mister assures us.

"How big is the camp?" Brother Dominic asks.

"It's about twenty by thirty. It has two upstairs bunk rooms," he answers.

"Is it close to a body of water?" Ralph asks.

"Yes," Mr. Mister answers. "It's on an island."

Chapter 4

Shopping Spree

Most of us got a decent night's sleep. We begin piling into our van, ready to begin the journey to our island camp. Texas is in a particularly good mood. Mr. Mister supplied him with two firearms: a 12-gauge shotgun and a 30-30 rifle. Texas hides the guns under a seat along with a duffle bag filled with ammunition. As I put the van into drive, Mr. Mister walks up to my window.

"If anything changes, I'll try to get up there and let you know. Take care, Father," he ends.

"Thanks for everything, Mr. Mister," I reply.

***

Back on the country road, I can't help but feel nervous again. If we get pulled over by the police, they might be looking for us. I make sure to drive the speed limit and pray.

We need supplies for our stay at the camp. We decide to purchase as much gear and as many supplies as possible since we may have to spend the winter on the island.

When we get to the last village before the wilderness, we are all shocked at how small it is. The village has a gas station with a corner store and a little outfitter store.

"You gotta be kidding me," Ralph comments.

I park the van by the outfitters. Walking into the store we are greeted by a clerk. "Good morning!" he says with a kind smile. The store happens to be well stocked with the items we need.

Each one of us selects a sleeping bag, warm clothing, winter boots, and just about every other item you could think of. Ralph, Texas, and I are treating our time of shopping as though it were a military operation, moving quickly and making sure we don't miss any essential items. Dominic is distracted, flipping through a book on local birds.

Christie is trying on a parka and examining her appearance in a mirror. "What do you think, Sister? Should I go with the red one?" she asks Mother Elijah. "The blue is nice, but I think I prefer the red," she adds as she turns to the left and pulls up the hood to admire herself in the mirror.

"Wearing red will make you an easy target," Mother Elijah responds as she compares the patterns on different scarves.

Thankfully, the deposit bag from the conference contains mostly large bills and we have no problem paying for the purchase with cash.

Next, we drive to the corner store attached to the gas station to see what kind of supplies it has. As we walk into the store, a tall, thin, middle aged man and an older, short woman are standing behind the checkout counter. They completely ignore us. Mother Elijah kindly asks them if they have rice, beans, and flour.

"In the back!" the woman responds, as she watches the *News Nation* morning talk show. I walk with Mother Elijah to the back of the store, and we finally locate some large bags of rice and a few dozen bags of other staples.

"Oh, this is perfect!" Mother Elijah exclaims.

The checkout lady begins scanning the growing pile of items being placed on the counter as the gentleman bags them. Both workers continue to watch the talk show and ignore us. Dominic notices the chocolate section and takes every single chocolate bar on the rack. Ralph notices Dominic's actions and proceeds to do the same with the chips, mixed nuts, and other snacking food. Soon some of the racks of the little store have been completely emptied. We purchase all the toilet paper.

When I finally pay the bill, I notice that we've almost completely emptied the store of its stock. We linger a little, making sure we haven't forgotten any essential items.

Suddenly the talk show is interrupted with a news update from the Canadian Prime Minister. He begins by thanking everyone for their calm during this time of communications failure. He gives an update on the progress of getting the systems back up. "I can assure you, cell phones will be working by tomorrow, maybe even later tonight," he says.

Meanwhile, I notice that the lady at the cash is scanning a case of Budweiser beer that Texas has placed on the counter. I'm appalled. This is not a necessary item, and why would someone purchase American beer when there is the far superior Canadian beer readily available? Ralph notices the beer and makes his way to the cooler, returning with a case of Bud Light. Now I'm offended. I react by going to the cooler myself and grabbing a case of Moosehead beer.

The beer is packed, along with the other supplies. The Prime Minister's speech is winding down.

"As you know, this communications failure will cause some distribution challenges in many parts of Canada, especially the most rural areas. We ask retailers to please offer vital products such as food and toilet paper in limited quantities so that there will be enough for everyone."

The two cashiers, who have ignored us the whole time, turn to look at us now. Their eyes wander over the empty shelves. I can't help a quick glance at the shelves myself. Then I notice my friends are already out the door and piling into the van. I don't dare look at the cashiers as I follow after them. We slam the side door of the van shut and peel off.

***

For a few minutes there is a stunned silence in the van. Then Christie begins to wave her hands. "Oh, this is not funny!" She covers her mouth with one hand and continues to wave her other hand. "Did you see the look on that cashier's face?" she exclaims. "This is not funny!" she says again, and then bursts into hysterical laughter. After a long fit, she eventually calms down. We are all amused as she wipes away her tears. The nice thing is that Christie's laughter manages to break so much of the tension we have been carrying for the last two days.

I begin to look forward to settling into our camp and feeling safe again. As we come out of a bend on the road onto a straight stretch, I behold the one thing I dreaded to see: three police cars stopped on the road with their lights flashing!

Chapter 5

Ice Cold

My heart sinks. "Ay, caramba!" I say. Everyone looks on in silent horror.

I take my foot off the accelerator and consider my options. All I can do is pray and keep driving. I continue to slow down, feeling complete hopelessness.

"It's over," I think to myself.

We drive along toward the police cars. My heart is pounding. I begin to imagine what life will be like in a concentration camp. Ralph begins to speak in Latin. It sounds like he's performing an exorcism.

The police car that was blocking the road slowly begins to move forward and drives to the left side of the road. A police officer standing on the right shoulder of the road steps onto the side of the road and waves.

Suddenly, I notice a car in the ditch on the right side of the road. The police officer continues to wave me along, indicating that I am to keep going. As we drive by, the waving officer seems impatient that I have slowed down so much and continues to wave, indicating that I should hurry up and keep going. None of the other officers even look at us.

I keep driving, accelerating very gradually. Christie starts up with her two hands over her face. "Oooooooh! Oooooooh!" she cries.

Ralph's eyes are closed. He has a look of tremendous relief. Texas is holding on to the seat in front of him, looking forward, eyes and mouth wide open. Mother Elijah has two pillows pressed against each side of her head, hiding her face. Brother Dominic is reading his bird book.

***

After a long stretch of reflective silence, Mother Elijah suggests we pray a rosary together in thanksgiving and for God's protection. No one objects. Mother asks me if I would like to lead the rosary. I decline. "You go for it, Sister," I say.

She agrees and begins by making the Sign of the Cross. "In the Name of the Father, and of the Son, and of the Holy Spirit. Amen." Mother Elijah prays each prayer calmly and slowly. You can tell she has cultivated the habit of praying from the depths of her heart. It is beautiful; everyone in the van, covered in rolls of toilet paper, winter clothing, and pillows, responds to each prayer in unison. Except for Ralph; he responds in Latin.

***

The van rolls along deeper and deeper into the wilderness. We take one last turn onto a rough and narrow road. The van scratches against branches that have grown into the side of the road. A few times, Ralph and Texas have to get out of the van to help me navigate our vehicle through washed out sections and around mud holes and rocky stretches. We press on a long time like this as the van engine and transmission begin to overheat.

"No one's going to find us here," Brother Dominic observes.

The sky begins to grow dark, and we are still looking for an abandoned dump truck next to a wooden bridge that Mr. Mister told us about. Finally, we spot the bridge and the old dump truck. Ralph has to get out of the van one last time to make sure my wheels are lined up properly on the old wooden planks which cross over a swiftly flowing creek. A few minutes later I park the van in a little clearing next to a beautiful lake. We wearily crawl out of the van and admire the calm water. There is a small island in the distance, with a little cabin near the shore. The cabin has a covered veranda that faces the lake, a chimney, and a shed behind it.

"Oh, this is Heaven!" Christie exclaims.

"It's so peaceful," Mother Elijah adds.

Texas walks up to us with a beer in his hand. "Anyone want a beer?" he asks. Everyone declines, so he twists the top off and takes a swig.

We all take in the stillness of the place. Brother Dominic breaks the silence with a simple question: "So how do we get to the island?"

The thought never even crossed my mind.

"Shouldn't there be a boat or something here?" Ralph asks. We look around everywhere for a boat or canoe or anything to cross over to the island but find nothing.

"There seems to be a canoe next to the shed on the island," Texas notices.

"Could someone swim over there?" Dominic asks.

"No. It's October. The water is freezing cold and it's a long distance. You'd get hypothermia," I reply. "We can spend the night in the van," I say. "Tomorrow we can figure out a way to cross over to the island."

We all stand in disappointed silence as the reality of spending a night in the van sinks in.

Texas shakes his head. He passes his bottle to Christie and says: "Hold my beer."

Chapter 6

Island Time

Texas strips down to his boxer shorts and begins to wade into the water. "Cold! Cold! Cold!" he exclaims as he walks stubbornly into the wilderness lake.

"That's not a good idea," I say, my voice rising in concern.

"C'mon man, don't be foolish," Ralph says.

"No, Texas! This is not necessary!" Mother Elijah adds.

Texas dives into the water and disappears. When he finally surfaces a surprising distance away, he lets out a scream: "Whooeeeeee! It's cold!" Then he begins to swim energetically towards the island. We watch him make his way little by little towards his destination. Within a short time, Texas is stumbling out of the water onto the shore of the island.

"Whoooooooeeeeee! Yeaaaaaah! Whoooooop! Feels great!" he exclaims.

A minute later he is climbing into the canoe and paddling his way back to us. We are all deeply relieved, firstly that Texas is still alive and secondly that we have a watercraft in which to ferry across to the island.

Texas approaches us with a huge smile on his face. He is beaming. I steady the canoe for him so that he can get out. Mother Elijah hands him a towel from the van and Christie returns his beer.

"I suggest we take what we need for the night. We can come back for the rest tomorrow," I say. All agree.

"Maybe Sister and I could arrange the camp while you guys ferry whatever items we need for our first night," Christie suggests.

"Sounds good," Ralph responds.

I volunteer to paddle the two ladies to the camp as the guys start sorting through the supplies in the van to decide what we will need for the night.

Both ladies settle themselves shakily into the canoe and we begin our crossing. We almost tip the canoe as the ladies disembark. Christie provides plenty of sound effects. She races excitedly to the cottage as Mother Elijah follows her at a more sensible pace. I pull the canoe onto the little beach.

"Mr. Mister said the key is on the top sill of the left window," I remind Christie.

"Found it!" she calls back and goes in.

As I walk toward the cabin, there is a moment of silence and then a loud scream. Christie continues to scream in horror and Mother Elijah begins to increase her pace toward the cabin. Christie runs out of the cabin still screaming. "There's a mouse in the cabin!" she announces to every creature within a ten-mile radius.

I can hear Ralph and Texas laughing in the distance. It's at this point that I realize that my new providentially appointed community is going to come with its own challenges.

***

I paddle the empty canoe back to the van and the men already have a plan. Texas will stay at the van and help load the canoe. I will ferry the gear across. Brother Dominic and Ralph will help unload the gear and lug it into the cabin.

***

It's starting to get dark. Texas and I are canoeing to the camp with the last load of supplies for the night. The surface of the lake is smooth like a mirror.

"Can I ask you a question?" I ask Texas.

"What's up, Father Pedro?" he says.

"Everyone knows that Ralph has been speaking out against the New World Order, but why would the Globies be after the rest of you?" I ask.

Texas chuckles. "We've all been bad-talking the Globies," he says. "Christy hasn't been shy to rant against the global elite in some of her articles, and I was doing the same in my YouTube videos," he explains.

"What about Mother Elijah and Brother Dominic?" I ask. "They don't seem like the types to criticize the secular powers," I say.

"Oh, Mother Elijah was the worst!" Texas exclaims. "Have you ever heard any of her talks? I remember hearing her give a teaching on contemplative prayer. It was the most beautiful talk on prayer I'd ever heard. She ended her talk by sweetly reminding everyone that we were living in the End Times and that the spirit of the Antichrist was now here. She called the New World Order the 'Great Rebellion.' She didn't mince words."

"What about Brother Dominic?" I ask.

"I've never heard Dominic speak out against the Globies," Texas says. "What I do know is that there is a group of bishops along with some Catholic scholars who have written statements of concern regarding the ideologies driving the New World Order. Brother Dominic's was almost always one of the signatures on those statements. His signature means a lot because Dominic is very well-known and respected," Texas says.

I continue to paddle the canoe as I ponder the gravity of our situation.

"Sorry for getting you into this mess Father," Texas says.

"It's all good," I reply.

***

Texas and I get to the shore with our final load of supplies. We have everything we need for our first night. Everyone is exhausted but relieved. Mother Elijah and Christie managed to cook a delicious meal while we were ferrying the supplies to the island. There is a fire in the wood stove and some candles light up our new home.

As we gather around the table, it is obvious that Mother Elijah and Brother Dominic are into table etiquette. Our first meal together in our rustic hunt camp is spent feasting in the most civilized manner.

***

Completely exhausted, I crawl into my sleeping bag. There are two rooms upstairs. The ladies take one room and Texas, Ralph, and I share the other. Brother Dominic sleeps on an old couch on the main floor.

***

"Nada te turbe, solo Dios, basta."

The sound of a woman gently singing draws me out of a deep sleep. It's morning. I immediately remember the awful predicament we are in, hiding from the Globies on an island in the wilderness.

The sound of Mother Elijah's song catches my attention again. *"Nada te turbe,"* she sings. Don't let anything trouble you. I make the sign of the cross and think of some things I am thankful for before I begin my day. I think immediately of Mother Elijah. She's probably one of the holiest people I've ever met, and here she is singing in the room below me. I think of Christie and how delightfully amusing she is. I thank the Lord for Mother Elijah and Christie. Then I think of Texas swimming across the lake, hooting and hollering after he made it across. His daring spared us a lot of misery. I thank the Lord for Ralph and Brother Dominic too. Joy fills my spirit. I marvel at how a few moments of thanksgiving can have such a powerful effect on me.

***

"Good morning, Sister," I say to our camp cook. "Good morning, Father," she replies. I notice that Mother Elijah is making some kind of porridge. Still a little sleepy, I look out the big window at our pristine wilderness view. Clouds of fog move across the placid lake. All is still as I look at the old wooden dock, the little sand beach, the ... "Where's the canoe?!"

Chapter 7

Need Coffee

"The canoe?" Sister asks.

"It's gone!" I tell her. She leaves her porridge and comes to look out the window.

"Did someone take it?" she asks.

I look at the couch. "Where's Dominic?" Then I notice in the distance a canoe zigzagging along the shore towards us.

It takes a long time for Dominic to finally make it back to the camp. I go to the beach to help him disembark from the canoe. He looks awful.

"What happened to you?" I ask.

His hair is disheveled, one of his pant legs is rolled up to his knee and the other is soaking wet. There's a scrape on his arm that's bleeding. He lifts four beer bottles from the bottom of the canoe. Each bottle is filled with water and has a grocery bag stuffed in the top.

"Coffee," he tells me.

Back in the camp, Dominic is not answering any of the questions Sister and I ask him. He scurries around and finds a small pot. He rips the plastic bag out of the top of the beer bottle and pours the water into the pot. He places the pot on the wood stove and begins scurrying around the kitchen again. Mother Elijah opens a cupboard and calmly removes a bag of coffee and places it on the counter.

"It's okay, Dominic," she gently assures the young intellectual.

Fifteen minutes later, Dominic begins to speak. "Mr. Mister said there was a spring with good water in the far bay, so when I woke up this morning, I decided to get some for my coffee. I don't trust the lake water." He takes another sip of his coffee and then continues, "I couldn't find any jugs for carrying water, so I decided to use the empty beer bottles. I don't function well until I've had my morning coffee. And I had some challenges," he says as he looks at the scrape on his arm. He takes another sip of coffee. "Where's my chocolate?" he asks.

***

Texas is the last one to get up. After we've all had breakfast and some of Dominic's finely brewed coffee, we talk about what needs to be done this day. "I'm going fishing," Texas states.

"I might do an inventory of what useful items we have in the shed next door and around the camp," Ralph shares.

"I have no plans," Dominic informs us.

"Were you going to celebrate Mass today, Father?" Mother Elijah asks me.

"Yes, I'd love to," I tell her. One thing I made sure to grab before leaving my rectory was a Mass kit.

"Let's have some charismatic praise with the Mass," Christie says excitedly waving her arms in the air. "If you want the power, you need to praise the Lord!" she proclaims to us.

"There needs to be at least some Latin and the Holy Sacrifice of the Mass should be celebrated *ad orientem*," Ralph insists.

"The Mass is meant to be prayed. It should be celebrated with simplicity. It should help lead us into contemplation," Mother Elijah tells us.

"As long as there's some intellectual substance in the homily, I'm happy," says Dominic.

"And keep the homily short," Texas adds.

"Actually," I respond, "that's exactly how all my Masses are celebrated: *ad orientem*, with charismatic praise and lots of Latin. Done with prayerful simplicity leading everyone into contemplation. And always a short homily full of intellectual substance."

Everyone seems satisfied, so we agree that we will have Mass together before dinner.

***

Over the next few days, the reality of our new circumstances begins to sink in. Christie cries almost every day and Mother Elijah is sometimes seen with tears in her eyes. Ralph seems fairly content. He spends a lot of his day picking through the junk in the shed.

Texas, on the other hand, is like a kid at summer camp. He goes fishing, takes hikes, usually with the shotgun and hoping to find some game, makes campfires, and is crazy enough to take the occasional swim. He reminds us over and over again how much he regrets that he had to destroy his phone. This adventure would provide great content for his YouTube channel, he tells us.

Dominic fills the empty beer bottles with spring water three times a day. We all appreciate his coffee and the bottles of fresh spring water. We all marvel at how wonderful the spring water tastes.

I'm exhausted and mainly poke around the camp and ask Dominic theological questions. Sister and Christie continue to arrange the kitchen and work hard at cooking and cleaning.

***

We've been here for close to a week now and things are pretty chill. Dominic and I are enjoying an afternoon coffee and we begin to discuss Cicero's understanding of the best form of governance. Ralph joins us and begins to criticize Norway's constitutional monarchy. Texas walks in, grabs a bag of chips and a beer, and immediately starts challenging Ralph's opinions of Norway's parliamentary system. I mention how Canada's parliamentary system works and everyone ignores me. Dominic humbly informs both Ralph and Texas that they don't know what they're talking about. Ralph reminds Dominic that his liberal ideas don't take into account the pattern of hierarchy established by God and reflected in all creation and also in the Heavenly order. Texas reminds Ralph that God is a God of diversity and that God doesn't just understand Latin. I'm about to mention Canada's Fathers of Confederation when I notice Mother Elijah and Christie standing right in front of us. Sister is not smiling. She hands her bottle of water to Christie and tells her, "Hold my beer."

"Our God," Sister begins with a calm and measured severity, "is a God of order and SILENCE! Perhaps, rather than debating the merits of Norway's current administration," she continues, "you could figure out some kind of governance at this camp that will ensure that the men are doing their fair share of the work around here." Sister takes her bottle from Christie and goes back to scrubbing a pot. Christie's eyes bulge out as she looks at us. She seems shocked and thrilled over Mother Elijah's unexpected scolding.

After a long pause, Dominic says, "I propose that we elect a General Superior after dinner tonight."

Chapter 8

Dictator for Life

Dinner is a little tense, knowing that we are about to hold an election. Dominic is the most composed and seems assured that the proceedings will run smoothly.

"What smells so good?" Texas asks.

"Sister made a banana loaf," Christie responds.

"Oh, I can't wait," Ralph says. "What a good way to get ready to elect a new leader."

"The banana loaf will be served after the election. To celebrate the establishment of civility on our new island state," Mother Elijah clarifies.

"It's so that we can get this over with quickly," Christie adds. "We don't care about Cicero and the Norwegian political system. If someone wants to start debating about ancient Greek philosophy and political theory, they're the one responsible for making us all wait for dessert," she warns.

***

After dinner, Dominic begins to prepare for the proceedings. He moves the furniture around so that the couch and three chairs are facing the kitchen table. Dominic places one wooden chair behind the table and then disappears upstairs. The room looks like a little classroom. We are the students and Dominic, it would appear, will be the teacher. Sister takes the banana loaf out of the oven, filling the camp with its wonderful aroma. We all take it as a reminder not to waste time. Christie serves tea. Dominic reappears walking down the stairs in his full Dominican habit. There is a hushed silence as Dominic takes up his position as presider of the event.

"Tonight, we will elect a leader," he solemnly begins. "The current practice in the Roman Catholic Church is to recommend that newly established institutes adopt an elected form of governance with a limited term. The leader is to work with a council according to the constitutions of the institute. The councilors are also to be elected," Dominic explains. "If everyone is in agreement, we can begin with the proceedings."

"Fine," Ralph says.

"First, we need to have a time of open dialogue concerning the suitability of the various candidates," says Dominic. "We need to determine who would be best suited for the important role of leader. This way, we can vote with an informed understanding of the strengths and weaknesses of each candidate," he explains.

"Well, I think the priest should be the leader," Ralph informs us.

"I agree, let's just go with a good old-fashioned theocracy," says Texas.

"Nope, no way!" I respond. "I'm not a leader," I state.

"You're not a leader?" Christie says. "If you're a priest, you have to be a leader. How can you run a parish if you're not a leader?" Christie asks.

"Most parishes are run by a good secretary," I explain. "I think Ralph would be our best leader," I suggest. "He's spent his whole career criticizing leadership. Let's give him an opportunity to show this island what the perfect leader looks like," I say.

"No way!" Christie responds. "The last thing this island needs is a ruthless dictator. Mother Elijah should be our leader. She is the holiest and the wisest person on the island."

"No, I'm not at all cut out for worldly leadership," Mother Elijah replies. "My calling is to a life of prayer and contemplation. Temporal matters should be the concern of a lay person."

"What about Dominic?" Texas suggests. "He seems to know about ruling with proper order and justice."

"I agree with Sister — as a religious brother I don't feel it's proper for me to be concerned about affairs of the state," Dominic answers.

"Christie, didn't you graduate from law school?" Dominic asks.

"Maybe," Christie hesitantly responds.

"You're a lawyer?" Texas says. "I thought you were a journalist."

"I graduated from law school and then went on to journalism. Either way, I'm not going to be made responsible for managing you guys. No way!" Christie declares.

"I guess that leaves you, Texas," Ralph says. "I'm sure your career as a YouTuber has helped you develop all of the skills necessary to rule your own nation," he says.

"Nope. I need to be able to focus all my time and energy on fishing and hunting. This island doesn't just need leadership. It also needs food," he insists.

Christie scoffs. "How many fish have you caught so far? None! And how many animals did you shoot? None!"

"Order! Order!" Dominic says, tapping his teaspoon on the table. "Now that we have discussed our leadership options, we are ready to vote," Dominic tells us.

"A majority vote will be required," Dominic says. "There are six of us. The elected leader requires at least four votes."

Pieces of paper are distributed, and we are instructed by Dominic to write clearly. Each one of us scribbles a name on our paper, and then places the folded paper into a salad bowl on the corner of Dominic's table.

Mother Elijah is the last one to place her ballot into the bowl.

"We will now read the names out loud and count the votes," Dominic explains. "I will need two people to verify each vote," he says. "Perhaps Texas and Christie could assist at this task?" Dominic asks.

With Christie sitting at his right and Texas at his left, Dominic reads the first name: "Father Pedro." Dominic shows the slip to Christie. She nods. Then he shows the slip to Texas. He too nods.

Dominic pulls out the next slip of paper. "Brother Dominic." Christie and Texas verify the name.

The next four slips have Mother Elijah's name written on them and she is officially the winner of the election. There is a little round of applause and Sister shyly waves to us.

Dominic quiets the little crowd and asks Mother Elijah, "Mother Elijah, do you accept?"

She hesitates and then responds, "I do." There is another round of applause.

Dominic continues, "Now we must elect members to serve on the leadership council."

"Do we have to?" asks Texas.

"Yes, why does Sister need a council?" Christie asks.

"I agree," Ralph adds as he looks towards the banana loaf.

"We can't have a leader without some form of council," Dominic responds. "There has to be accountability. Otherwise, we would be pretty much dealing with a dictatorship," he warns.

"Yes, but Mother Elijah would be a benevolent dictator," I counter as I too gaze towards the banana loaf.

Dominic hesitates and then sighs. "Fine. There is one last order of business. We need to determine the length of Mother's term."

"We'd better not be on this island for four years!" Christie cries out.

"We're hopefully only here for a few months," I say.

"I'm guessing we'll be spending the winter here," says Texas.

"She doesn't need a term," Ralph insists. "Let's just say that Sister is in charge as long as we're on this island together." Everyone seems to agree.

Dominic shrugs and then says, "Very well, we are all in agreement. Sister will be our dictator for life." There is another little round of applause.

"Sister," I ask, "as our new leader, what are your first words to your people?"

"Let's have dessert!" she replies.

***

There is great joy in the camp as we celebrate with the delicious banana bread. Despite being fugitives hiding from the Globies, we are able to enjoy a little celebration together.

"This is really exciting," Texas says as he helps himself to another slice of banana bread. "I never thought I would be one of the founding fathers of a newly established island state."

"Yes, we just formed a new government," I add.

"Since we are pretty much sharing everything in common and no one runs a business or is making any money, does that make us a communist state?" Christie asks.

"Yes," Dominic answers. "We've just established a communist dictatorship."

***

I go to bed feeling well fed and hopeful that all will be well on our little island. My head hits the pillow and I feel myself drift off into a wonderful dream land.

***

Suddenly, I am awakened from a deep sleep by the sound of a loud, revving engine. It's dark and I'm freezing cold. I crawl out of my sleeping bag confused and afraid. I look out the window and see what appears to be spotlights on the lake scanning the shoreline.

Chapter 9

Freeze

"They found us," I mutter out loud as my sleepy eyes try to focus on the mysterious spectacle. Two bright lights scan the shore and then point to the north end of the lake. I see a red light on the lake, and then another one.

"What? It can't be!" I say in amazement. My face is so close to the window that my breath causes it to fog up. I rush downstairs, find some shoes and a jacket and walk out into the cold.

I can hardly believe what I see. The lake is covered with ice, and someone is in our van spinning in circles on the frozen water.

"What is going on?" I say as I stumble toward the frozen shore.

The van comes to a stop and then begins to slowly roll towards me. The headlights are shining on me, and I can't make out who's driving.

"Hey, Father," Texas says through the open window. "Need a lift?"

"Dude, are you crazy?" I say. "You could go through. This isn't safe."

"Actually, I checked the ice. It's fine. I watched a TV show about trucks driving on ice roads in Alaska. People do this kind of stuff all the time."

***

The sky is just beginning to lighten up and I realize that it's early morning. The lake is indeed covered with a thick layer of ice. Growing up in Canada, I've learned to appreciate the rare year in which the temperature would suddenly drop on a calm, windless night. The next morning, the lakes and ponds would be covered with a smooth layer of ice. As kids, we would go out and skate on these natural skating rinks. This was one such year. There is still no snow on the ground, but the lake is frozen solid.

"You know that every frozen lake has thin patches, right?" I ask Texas. "If you drive over one of those you're going through. There are springs and currents of water below the surface. You need to be careful." Texas remains silent. "Beautiful, isn't it?" I add.

***

After breakfast, everyone is out on the ice. I walk alongside Ralph, who is not at all steady on the slippery ice. Christie and Sister walk together arm in arm. Dominic appears to be making his way to the spring. Texas is exploring the far side of the lake. I'm amazed at how clearly you can see the bottom of the lake through the ice. It seems like I can look down as deep as twelve or fourteen feet. I continue to walk, marveling at the rocks and weeds, when I notice something moving.

"A fish," I say, pointing down. "Look at the fish," I say to Ralph.

***

Within a short time, we have a hole in the ice and a line in the water. One of the things Ralph found while he was rummaging through the shed was an ice auger. Now he is putting it to good use. We all gather around as Ralph slowly lets a line down through the freshly cut hole. Ralph then begins to tug on the line in a rhythmic fashion. We all watch with utter fascination and great anticipation. After thirty seconds, Dominic and Christie begin to get restless. Two minutes later, Ralph is still jigging the line as we all begin to leave. "Well, good luck with that, Ralph," Texas says, as we all walk away.

A moment later we hear Ralph's excited voice. "Fish on!" We all turn around and see Ralph quickly pulling the line up, and suddenly out of the hole appears a flopping fish. "Walleye!" Ralph exclaims.

***

I top up my coffee as Dominic explains to me what differentiates the Dark of Night of the Spirit from the Dark Night of the Senses, according to the mystical theology of St. John of the Cross. Mother Elijah and Christie listen attentively to Dominic's sublime teaching. The ladies are enjoying some tea as they prepare the evening dinner. Dominic takes a sip of water from his recycled beer bottle and continues his discourse. The divine teaching is interrupted when Ralph barges into the cabin holding a stringer full of fish.

"Bring me a knife," he calls out, his face red from being out in the cold for a few hours.

A cutting board is located. "I got this," I announce and proceed to gut one of the fish.

"No, no!" Ralph says. "These are walleye — they need to be filleted," he tells me.

Texas walks in as Ralph begins to make a mess out of a second fish. "Dude, let me show you how to do that," he tells Ralph.

Texas grabs a third fish and begins scraping the scales off of it, sending shiny little flakes of smelly fish scales all over the counter and beyond. The kitchen counter is turned into a slimy mess of hacked up fish, with guts, blood and scales everywhere. Christie's jaw drops at the spectacle. She is left in a rare state of speechlessness.

Sister is about to raise her voice in protest to the massacre that is taking place in her kitchen when suddenly Dominic steps in.

"Hold my beer," he tells Christie.

Christie reacts still half in shock, taking the bottle of water into her hand. Dominic walks up to the kitchen counter, his back straight, knife in his right hand. He begins by rapidly scraping the knife a few times against a sharpening stone he finds in a drawer.

He takes one of the fish and lays it on its side. He then makes a small cut on one side of the gills. He flips the walleye over and does the same on the other side. Then with one steady cut, he removes the flesh from the side of the fish. He places the fillet skin down and in one swipe removes the skin from the fillet. The whole process takes about fifteen seconds, and there is no mess.

"This is another way of doing it," Dominic tells us.

***

That evening we feast on the most delicious fish I've ever tasted in my whole life. Dominic shares that his religious community owns a retreat house in northern Saskatchewan where he has spent many summers. "The friars would go fishing almost every day, and the rule was that the youngest friar had to clean the fish," Dominic tells us.

"This batter is perfect—better than any restaurant," Christie comments. "What's your secret recipe?" she asks Mother Elijah.

"Pancake mix," she responds.

***

As we finish our meal, Christie brings a plate of fresh-baked chocolate chip cookies to the table. We all dig in.

"Something happened to me on the ice today," Ralph says, holding a cookie in his hand. "It's like I was able to see the beauty in everything. It seemed like God had made everything just for me. It felt so peaceful. For a few moments, I knew in the depths of my soul that God the Father really does love me, and I really am His son. All my fears and worries just disappeared," he continues. "It felt like a premonition or something," he shares pensively.

***

After dishes, Mother Elijah brews a pot of mint tea. Texas opens the door of the wood stove so we can admire the fire as we enjoy our tea together.

"The frozen lake is so cool," Texas says.

"Yesterday I was exploring the other side of the beaver

56

dam and discovered a long, winding channel of water. The frozen channel is about the width of a sidewalk, and it seems to go on for miles through swampy grasslands. I walked for over an hour marveling at the smoothness of the ice. Just like Ralph described, I felt so peaceful. It's like I would have been content following that enchanted path forever and ever."

"I wish we had ice skates," Christie says.

"It's funny you should say that," Mother Elijah responds. "When I was a child, I watched the Winter Olympics with my older sisters," she says, holding her teacup with two hands. "My sisters loved to watch figure skating. That year, a beautiful young girl from Sweden won the gold medal. She was only sixteen years old. They showed on TV her little hometown where she would sometimes practice figure skating on an outdoor rink. I was dazzled by the wonder of figure skating. How serious yet free the athletes all were. They wore such lovely outfits and captivated the whole world's attention. They seemed to be doing something truly worthy of the dignity of a child of God.

"I would lie in bed at night and imagine myself living in a village where all the roads were frozen with beautiful smooth ice. Night after night, I would imagine skating up and down streets and through parks, sometimes with friends, sometimes alone, sometimes going long distances over a glassy sea.

"Today brought back those memories that so inspired me as a child. I began to wonder if perhaps the

Lord was letting me know that one day I will experience the fulfillment of this dream in Heaven."

"Do you think there will be figure skating in Heaven?" Christie asks Dominic.

We all sit quietly contemplating the fire. I begin to get drowsy and decide that I'm ready for bed when a jarring sound breaks the silence.

KNOCK, KNOCK.

Someone is at our door!

Chapter 10

Treasure Chest

All of us freeze at the sound of the loud pounding.

"Anybody home?" a voice calls out.

"It's Mr. Mister!" I say.

Mr. Mister walks in the door with a big smile on his face. "Well, look at these happy campers!" he exclaims.

***

Mr. Mister takes off his big parka and winter boots and takes a seat on the couch. Ralph twists the top off a beer bottle and hands it to our guest.

"Have you eaten?" Mother Elijah asks.

"I'm good, I'm good," he waves her off.

"Tell us what's new," I say.

He begins to shake his head. "It's not good. Not good," he tells us. He goes on to recount how only the mainstream media sources are able to broadcast on the internet, TV, and radio. The government keeps assuring people that the new global communication network will be open to all content producers shortly, but no one believes them. He adds that there have been reports of conflicts in many parts of the world. The media barely makes any mention of these things. Mr. Mister says he knows people with shortwave radios who are hearing information that is not being broadcast by the mainstream media.

"The constant report on the shortwave is that people who oppose the Globies are being arrested and sent to concentration camps," Mr. Mister tells us. "A writer for our local newspaper disappeared three weeks ago after he wrote an article suggesting that the military is detaining people and even carrying out operations against resistance movements. Fred from the tire shop says he saw the journalist being led into a van, wearing handcuffs," our guest continues grimly. "You're probably best to stay here for a little longer," he tells us.

Mr. Mister rises to his feet. "Well, gotta go," he announces.

"No, you can't go back out into the cold and dark," Mother Elijah says. "You should stay the night."

"Nope. It's best I travel in the dark so that no one figures out what I'm up to," he tells us. "I wanted to get up here before the snow falls so I wouldn't leave any tracks," he adds. "You all pray for me, okay?" he asks us as he zips up his parka.

Texas leaves with Mr. Mister to walk him back across the lake, where his ATV has been parked out of sight.

"Well, it looks like we're spending the winter here," Dominic says.

***

After breakfast we are all back on the ice again. Dominic is pulling a homemade sled with a rope. In his sled is a box of beer bottles filled with hot chocolate. Dominic has been experimenting with hot chocolate recipes and has finally created a delicious winter drink. He proudly goes about handing each of us a bottle wrapped in cloth to keep the beverage warm. Ralph is excited about catching more fish and he is hard at work cutting new holes through the ice. He wants to try his luck in other spots. Christie and Mother Elijah are walking arm in arm along the shore of the lake.

The ice is as smooth as glass, and it still hasn't snowed. There is a beautiful blue sky with only a few clouds floating by. I ponder Mr. Mister's visit and the reality that we will have to spend the winter in this wilderness. I notice in the distance that Christie is down on her hands and knees. "Did she fall?" I think to myself. Then I notice Mother Elijah bending down as well. They seem to be looking at something below the surface of the ice.

I'm curious, so I begin to walk towards them. They start waving to the guys who are fishing. Dominic, Ralph, and Texas begin to walk toward the ladies.

"There's some kind of a chest down there," Christie tells us. Her face is almost against the frozen ice.

"It probably has a treasure in it," Texas suggests with a big smile.

I look through the ice and only see rocks, a few weeds, and some sunken logs. "I can't see it," I say.

"It's right there," Mother Elijah says.

I look more carefully but still can't see any treasure chest. "Where?" I ask.

"Between those two logs," Texas answers as he points in the direction that I've been looking towards.

"You guys are messing with me," I say.

"No. Look!" Christie insists.

I skeptically look again. "I see it!" I cry out.

***

Ralph and Texas show up with axes, saws, ropes, and other gear and begin cutting open the ice. The rest of us watch them as we enjoy our hot chocolate. They make an opening that's about four feet by four feet. Without hesitation, Texas strips down to his underwear and jumps into the ice-cold water.

"This guy is either super tough or completely insane," Ralph comments.

"Probably a combination of both," I reply.

Texas plunges down with a rope. We see him get within a short distance from the chest then resurface.

"It's deep," he tells us, gasping for air. He takes another deep breath and tries again. Once again, he can't quite make it to the sunken chest. After a third attempt, he finally gets out of the water.

"It's too deep," Texas tells us, breathing heavily. "There's no way we can get down there," he concludes.

There is a moment of disappointed silence and then all of a sudden Christie sighs, hands her hot chocolate to Texas and says, "Hold my beer."

She then proceeds to strip down to her long johns and jumps in the water.

"Christie!" Mother Elijah calls out in panic.

"It's cold! Oh, it's cold!" Christie says, as she treads water. She then reaches for the rope, takes a deep breath, and dives toward the chest.

We all watch in awe as she reaches the chest, carefully runs the ropes through the two side handles and ties a knot.

She double checks to see that the knot is tight. Gives the rope a little tug, takes one last look at the chest, and then looks up at us giving us a thumbs up.

When she finally surfaces, she once again reminds us of how cold the water is. Ralph and Texas help her onto the ice. Mother Elijah immediately covers Christie with her coat and we all stare at her in awe.

Shivering, she glances at us and notices our dropped jaws. "Captain of the water polo team," she informs us.

***

The chest is carefully lifted to the surface and onto the ice. Ralph and Texas try opening it but are not able to. We decide to slide it back to the island and try to open it there. "Whatever treasure is in that chest; I get half of it!" Christie playfully informs us.

Like a little band of pirates, we march back to the camp together, dragging our heavy chest behind us, ready to divide the spoils of today's exploits.

***

We drag the chest into the shed and Ralph pries it open with a crowbar. We all glance in and are disappointed that we are not dazzled by diamonds, gold coins, and precious jewels. Instead, all we see is half disintegrated clothing, a few rusted tools, and some pots and pans. Ralph is the most fascinated by the contents of the chest and carefully examines each tool. Christie looks disappointed and digs through the wet clothing and other items. "I risked my life for a bunch of soggy old clothing and rusty tools," she complains.

"And I held your hot chocolate for nothing," Texas adds.

"Oh, that was the best part," Christie replies. "That made it all worthwhile," she says as she continues to sort through the contents of the chest. "I can't tell you how good it felt telling someone to hold my beer. Why was I always the one holding someone's beer while they do something impressive? Mr. Mister makes me hold his beer while he shoots a wild turkey. Texas makes me hold his beer while he swims to the island. Sister makes me hold her beer while she scolds all of you. That was okay though. I'd hold Sister's beer anytime to watch her scold you guys again. Chef Dominic makes me hold his beer while he shows off his fish slicing skills. I was ready to punch the next person in the face who would dare tell me to hold his beer."

As Christie amuses us with her playful venting, she picks up a wooden box out of the chest and opens it. "Ohhhh!" she cries out. In her hands she holds a sparkling wine glass.

***

Back at the camp, we enjoy a mid-morning coffee break as we marvel at the six beautiful wine glasses Christie found in the box. Christie and Mother Elijah carefully cleaned each one of them and they are now placed as centerpieces on our dining table.

"They are definitely crystal," Dominic tells us.

"Is it just me, or does it seem a little weird that we just found six wine glasses and there are six of us hiding out at this camp?" Christie asks.

"We're all wondering the same thing," Ralph replies. "If you believe in Providence, this has to be more than a coincidence," he continues. We all stare in silence at the mysterious wine glasses.

"Well," Texas says, as he fixes his gaze out the window and reaches for his gun, "this is all very nice, but I've got some hunting to do."

Chapter 11

Burst of Love

Texas grabs the rifle and walks out the front door. We all rise to our feet and look out the large picture window.

"There it is," says Ralph as he points across the lake.

Along the shore is a massive bull moose standing in plain sight. We see Texas walking carefully towards the dock, gripping his firearm with his two hands. The moose lowers his nose to the ground and begins grazing. Suddenly, Texas begins to run back to the cabin. He runs up the steps, opens the door, and says: "Bullets! I need bullets!" Christie chuckles as Texas grabs a handful of bullets out of a little box next to the door. We all look out the window again and the moose is gone.

***

"We really could use some meat," Ralph comments as we enjoy a late lunch of rice and fish.

"We're really blessed to have a steady supply of fresh fish," I say.

"Yes, but fish every day is a bit much," Christie replies.

"I'm going to find that moose and pretty soon we're going to be eating some big steaks," Texas assures us.

"A moose chili would be nice," Dominic adds. "Or moose fried rice. Moose noodle soup. Moose roast. Moose burgers," he goes on.

"We do need to ration our food if we want to get through the winter," **Mother Elijah** reminds us.

***

Mid-afternoon coffee has now become a highlight of our day. Chocolate is always part of the ritual, and everyone is glad that Dominic cleaned out the store of its chocolate. Another part of our camp ritual is that each person always has a bottle of water at every meal and even coffee break. The spring water is absolutely delicious, and we are all drinking plenty of it.

As I take a sip of water from my beer bottle, I notice a very familiar sight: a partridge sitting on the lower branch of the pine tree just next to the veranda. It's a ruffed grouse, to be more precise. When I was young, my uncle and I hunted these birds every fall. "If there is one thing I know how to do, it's how to shoot a partridge," I think to myself.

This is my moment. Finally, I can speak the three great words. I shove my bottle against Ralph's chest and say to him, "Hold my beer."

I get up, pick up the 12-gauge shotgun propped up against the wall near the door, take three shells from a little ammunition box, and stealthily walk out onto the veranda. I point the barrel of the gun towards the bird's head and shoot. The bird turns its head left and right. Missed!

I rushed and never took the time to actually aim. But the grouse is still on the branch. I can't miss this second time. The bird is only ten or twelve feet away from me. I could almost hit him with a stick. I aim the gun and take a second shot. Another miss!

Now the feathered creature is getting fidgety, and he starts nervously moving his head in every direction. This is so embarrassing! I put a third shell into the chamber and aim as carefully as I possibly can. I breathe in, hold it, and then pull the trigger. The instant my finger grips the trigger, the partridge literally ducks his head. I can see the wind from the shot ruffle the top feathers of the fidgety creature. I miss again. Finally, the bird decides to fly away.

"Ohhhhhh!" I hear Christie screaming. Totally embarrassed, I walk back into the camp. Needless to say, my fellow fugitives took the whole spectacle in from the big window. Christie is on the couch in the fetal position. She looks like she's dying. Everyone is laughing. Ralph and Texas are the only two who seem to have any sympathy for me. They try to offer me some words of comfort, but every time they open their mouths they too can only burst into laughter. Ralph finally hands me back my bottle of water.

***

I finish my water as everyone takes their turn teasing me about my poor marksmanship. Everyone is smiling and I find myself filled with a wonderful joy and love for my fellow fugitives.

Mother Elijah suddenly hushes us and says, "Listen." It's the sound of doves. We all rise and look out the window. Three beautiful doves are on the bannister of the veranda. The shining sun in the clear sky makes them dazzling white.

My heart begins to be filled with an intense heat. Then I hear a high-pitched, roaring sound. A fighter jet flies over our little island, and in a burst of love my soul leaves my body.

Chapter 12

Glassy Sea

Heaven cannot be described. Words cannot express the inexpressible. It is a reality of bliss filled with delights no eye has seen and no ear has heard. And yet, Heaven is so natural. In the next life, humans are even more human — we are perfectly human. One word describes Heaven: Love. God is Love.

On planet earth, the mystery of Heaven lies hidden in plain sight in so many ways. A child in the womb has eyes but does not see, and ears but can hear only faintly. An unborn child has legs but is not yet able to skip and run. She has not yet seen her mother's face. Then, when the time is right, the child leaves the world of the womb. She passes through the mysterious door of the birth canal and enters into a whole new reality. In the world beyond the womb, a child experiences wonders that she could never have imagined while in the womb. When we pass through the mysterious door of death, a whole new reality opens.

It would be perfectly true to say that **Mother Elijah**'s dream of skating on a glassy sea, dressed in dazzling beauty to the sound of angelic music has indeed been fulfilled. Ralph enjoys perfect peace. The adventures continue for Texas in Paradise. Christie, Dominic, and I are also fully alive.

By the mercy of God, our little company of fugitive island dwellers, persecuted for the sake of righteousness, will always be able to share a drink together at the eternal banquet.

It is you who have stood by me in my trials;
and I confer a kingdom on you,
just as my Father has conferred one on me,
that you may eat and drink at my table
in my kingdom…

Luke 22:28–30
(*New American Bible*)

About the Author

Fr. Mark Goring grew up in Pembroke, Ontario, Canada. He joined the Companions of the Cross order of priests when he was 18 years old. He studied philosophy at the Dominican College and Theology at St. Paul's University in Ottawa. He was ordained a priest in 2002.

Fr. Mark has served as Associate Pastor of St. Mary's Parish in Ottawa, Director of Admissions for the Companions of the Cross, Chaplain to the Catholic Students at York University in Toronto, and Director of the Catholic Charismatic Center in Houston, Texas. He now serves as Pastor of St. Mary's Parish in Ottawa.

Fr. Mark contributes to Food for Life TV ministry and posts a daily video on his YouTube channel. He also enjoys spending time in the great outdoors.

Also by Fr. Mark Goring, CC

In His Zone
7 Principles for Thriving in Solitude

St. Joseph the Protector
A Nine-Day Preparation for Entrustment to St. Joseph

Printed in Great Britain
by Amazon

66778988R00050